PREPARATION FOR CITIZENSHIP

PROGRAM CONSULTANTS

Dolores Doran de Valdez
Director of Basic Education and Special Projects
Allan Hancock College
Santa Maria, California

Claudia Riedel
ESL Specialist
Palm Beach County School Board
Palm Beach County, Florida

Joe A. Burgos
ESL Instructor
Harris County Department of Education
Houston, Texas

STECK-VAUGHN ®
C O M P A N Y
ELEMENTARY • SECONDARY • ADULT • LIBRARY

Acknowledgments

Consultants

Dolores Doran de Valdez is Director of Basic Education and Special Projects at Allan Hancock College in Santa Maria, California. Ms. Valdez develops curriculum materials for both the preliteracy and beginning ESL levels. She holds a master's degree in Latin American literature from UCLA.

Claudia Riedel is an ESL specialist for the Palm Beach County School Board in Palm Beach County, Florida. She has authored citizenship curriculum materials for beginning and advanced ESL levels. Ms. Riedel also serves as a community liaison, working with local businesses and churches to set up ESL and literacy classes in Palm Beach County. Ms. Riedel received her master's degree in Educational Administration from McGill University.

Joe A. Burgos, an ESL instructor for ten years, works with ESL students at the Adult Learning Center in Houston. He has taught extensively at the preliterate level and holds a master's degree from Prairie View A & M. Mr. Burgos develops ESL materials for his own students as well as for many other preliteracy/beginning ESL programs in Harris County.

Staff Credits

Senior Editor: Beverly Anne Grossman
Design Manager: Sharon Golden
Photo Research: Margie Foster

Photo Credits

Unit Openers: #1 Stan Kearl; #2 Library of Congress; #3 UNIPHOTO/Ron Sherman; #4 © P. Gridley/FPG

P. 2 © Stock Imagery/Henyrk T. Kaiser; p. 4 © Obremski/Image Bank; p. 6 © Hutchings/PhotoEdit; p. 7 Stan Kearl; p. 8 © UNIPHOTO/Brady; p. 13, 13 Historical Pictures Service, Chicago; p. 13 Bettmann Archive; p. 14 Library of Congress; p. 15, 15 Historical Pictures Service, Chicago; p. 15 © John Neubauer; p. 16 © State Historical Society of Wisconsin; p. 18 © Anne Van Der Veer/Image Bank; p. 18 courtesy National Park Service; p. 20 © Harris & Ewing; p. 21 © Stock Imagery/John Feingersh; p. 22 © Curtis Willock/Image Bank; p. 22 © Stock Boston; p. 22 Stock Boston; p. 22 © Rentmeeseter/Image Bank; p. 23 © J.P. Laffont/Sygma; p. 23 Stan Kearl; p. 26 Sophia Smith Collection; p. 26 Valentine Museum; p. 26 Culver Pictures; p. 27 Bettmann Archive; p. 27 Sophia Smith Collection; p. 29 Brown Brothers; p. 30 Bettmann Archive; p. 30, 30 Library of Congress; p. 32 United States Army; p. 33 UPI Bettmann Newsphotos; p. 34 John F. Kennedy Library; p. 34 AP/Wide World; p. 34 UPI Bettmann Newsphotos; p. 35 UPI Bettmann Newsphotos; p. 35 United States Army; p. 38 H. Armstrong Roberts; p. 39 Bettmann Archive; p. 39 Library of Congress; p. 41 Stock Imagery; p. 42 © UNIPHOTO/Chris Cross; p. 43 Bettmann Archive; p. 43 H. Armstrong Roberts; p. 43 © UNIPHOTO/John Coletti; p. 45 Long Island State Park & Recreation Committee; p. 46 Bettmann Archive; p. 46 © State Historical Society of Wisconsin; p. 46 © Bob Fitch/Black Star; p. 46 UPI Bettmann Newsphotos; p. 48 © Mel Digiacomo/Image Bank; p. 48 Bettmann Archive; p. 53 AP/Wide World; p. 53 © John Neubauer; p. 55 UPI Bettmann Newsphotos; p. 56 © Gene Ahrens/FPG; p. 58 courtesy of Whitehouse; p. 58 Reuters/Bettmann; p. 59 courtesy of Whitehouse; p. 62 Supreme Court Historical Society; p. 63 Supreme Court Historical Society; p. 65 © Bob Daemmrich; p. 67 Rick Williams; p. 68 © Bob Daemmrich; p. 71 Reuters/Bettmann; p. 71 Reuters/Bettmann; p. 73 courtesy of Whitehouse.

ISBN 0-8114-7987-0

Contents

Unit 1 U.S. Symbols

Lesson 1 The U.S. Flag

The United States flag has fifty stars and thirteen stripes. There is a star for every state, including the states of Alaska and Hawaii.

Copy It Down

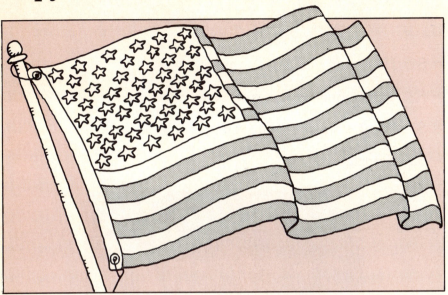

📝 **Copy the sentences.**

1. The United States began with thirteen colonies.

_____

_____

_____

2. The flag has thirteen stripes, one stripe for each colony.

_____

_____

_____

3. Now the United States has fifty states.

_____

_____

_____

4. The flag has fifty stars, one star for each state.

_____

_____

_____

Talk It Over

Dialogues: Practice with a partner.

- S1: How many colors are on the flag?
- ▶ S2: Three. Red, white, and blue.
- S1: What does the color red stand for?
- ▶ S2: Courage.

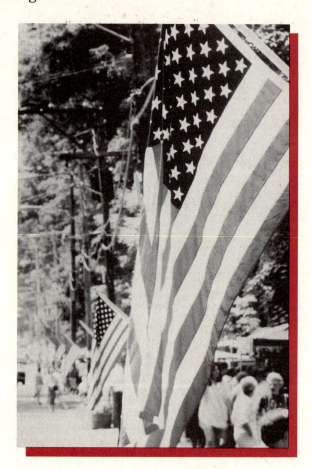

- S1: What's another word for *flag*?
- ▶ S2: Banner.
- S1: You mean like the "Star-Spangled Banner"?
- ▶ S2: Right. That's our national anthem.
- S1: What's an anthem?
- ▶ S2: It's a song.

Figure It Out

Circle the correct words.

1. The flag has fifty _____.

   stars   stairs

2. There are three colors on the flag.

   They are red, _____.

   white and black   white and blue

3. The U.S. flag has stars and _____.

   strips   stripes

Complete the dialogue using words from the box.
Write the correct answers. Then practice the
dialogue with a partner.

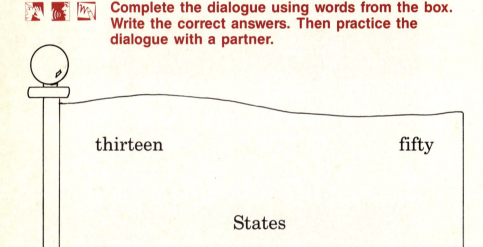

thirteen   fifty

                    States

colonies   flag

- S1: The flag is a symbol.

▶ S2: What for?

- S1: For the United _____.

▶ S2: Why are there _____ stripes?

- S1: Because there were thirteen _____.

▶ S2: Are there fifteen stars on the _____?

- S1: No, there are _____.

Lesson 2 Pledge of Allegiance

"I pledge allegiance to the flag of the United States of America, and to the Republic for which it stands, one Nation under God, indivisible, with liberty and justice for all."

Talk It Over

Read and discuss.

This man is saying the Pledge of Allegiance. He is promising to be loyal to the government of the United States. Americans face the flag when they say the Pledge of Allegiance because the flag is a symbol of our country.

Dialogue: Practice with a partner.

- S1: What does *indivisible* mean?
- S2: It means that the country can't be divided.
- S1: I know the word *liberty*.
- S2: So do I. It means freedom.
- S1: What does *justice* mean?
- S2: It means fairness.

Copy It Down

 Copy the sentences.

1. Americans say the Pledge of Allegiance while facing the flag. The flag is a symbol of the United States.

_____

_____

2. Americans promise to be loyal to the Republic which is the form of government in the United States.

_____

_____

3. The Pledge of Allegiance says that our nation is indivisible; it cannot be divided.

_____

_____

4. The Pledge of Allegiance also says that the United States is a nation of liberty and justice.

_____

_____

Figure It Out

Match the words with their correct meaning.

1. pledge   fairness

2. allegiance   loyalty

3. Republic   freedom

4. liberty   promise

5. justice   form of government

6. indivisible   cannot be divided

Fill in the blanks with the correct words from the box.

justice	indivisible	Republic
allegiance	pledge	liberty

"I _____ to the flag

of the United States of America, and to the

_____ for which it stands, one

Nation under God, _____, with

_____ and _____ for all."

Unit 2 U.S. History

Lesson 3

The Revolutionary War

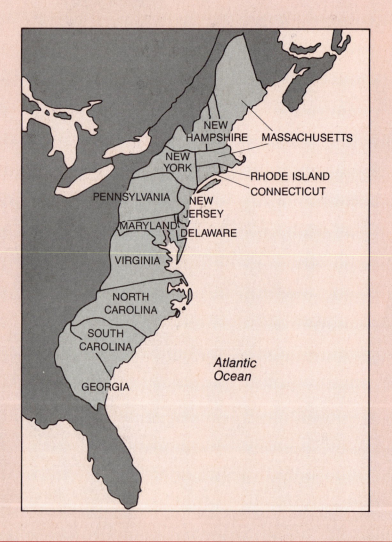

The United States began as 13 colonies ruled by England. The colonists were unhappy with English rule. They started the Revolutionary War in 1775 to gain their freedom.

Information

Read the sentences.

King George ruled England and the American colonies. The colonists did not like his laws.

The colonists had to pay high taxes on such things as sugar, tea, and paper. Colonists like Paul Revere thought these laws were unfair.

The colonists were willing to fight for their freedom. They wanted to establish their own government and to be independent from England.

Talk It Over

![dialogue icons] **Dialogues. Practice with a partner.**

- S1: How many terms did George Washington serve as president?
- ▶ S2: Two.
- S1: Can any president serve more terms than that?
- ▶ S2: No. It's against the law.

- S1: What special group advises the President?
- ▶ S2: The Cabinet.
- S1: Who created the Cabinet system?
- ▶ S2: George Washington.

Face to Face

Read the sentences.

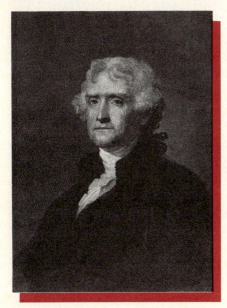

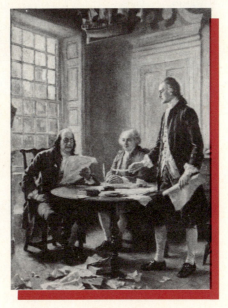

Thomas Jefferson was the third president of the United States. He was the principal writer of the Declaration of Independence. He wrote, "All men are created equal . . ."

Jefferson worked with John Adams and Benjamin Franklin to create the Declaration of Independence.

The Jefferson Memorial honors Thomas Jefferson. Many Americans visit this building each year. The Jefferson Memorial is in Washington, D.C.

Talk It Over

On July 4, 1776, many members of the Continental Congress signed the Declaration of Independence. Including Thomas Jefferson, John Adams, and Benjamin Franklin, there were 56 individuals who signed the document.

Dialogues: Practice with a partner.

- S1: What did the Declaration of Independence say?

▶ S2: It said that, as of July 4, 1776, the 13 colonies were free and independent of England.

- S1: Is this why July 4th is Independence Day?

▶ S2: Exactly. July 4th is "America's Birthday."

- S1: Who was Patrick Henry?

▶ S2: He was a member of the Continental Congress.

- S1: What did he do?

▶ S2: He said, "Give me liberty or give me death!"

Copy It Down

Copy the sentences.

1. The colonists were willing to fight for their freedom.

_____

_____

2. George Washington, our first president, created the
   Cabinet system.

_____

_____

3. The Declaration of Independence said the colonies were
   free from the government of England.

_____

_____

4. Thomas Jefferson was the principal writer of the
   Declaration of Independence.

_____

_____

_____

Extension

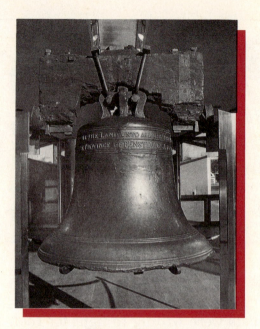

Liberty Bell

 Read and discuss.

On July 4, 1776, Americans rang the Liberty Bell to announce their independence. The Liberty Bell was rung at Independence Hall in Philadelphia, Pennsylvania. This was where many great Americans signed the Declaration of Independence.

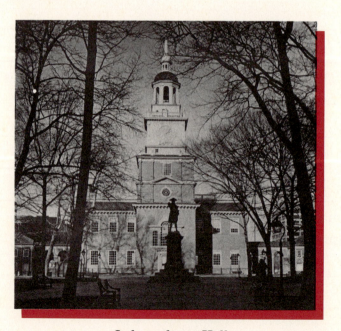

Independence Hall

Figure It Out

Complete the dialogue using words from the box. Write the correct answers. Then practice the dialogue with a partner.

Washington	Father
president	Revolutionary

- S1: By fighting the _____ War, Americans won freedom from England.

▶ S2: That's right.

- S1: George _____ led the Americans against the British.

▶ S2: Wasn't he also our first _____?

- S1: Yes, he is known as the "_____ of Our Country."

Complete the dialogue using words from the box. Write the correct answers. Then practice the dialogue with a partner.

England	Independence	Jefferson
equal	Declaration	

- S1: What was the Declaration of _____?

▶ S2: It said that the colonies were free from the government of _____.

- S1: Who was the principal writer of the _____ of Independence?

▶ S2: Thomas _____.

- S1: Didn't he write that "all men are created _____"?

▶ S2: Yes, he did.

Lesson 4 The Constitution

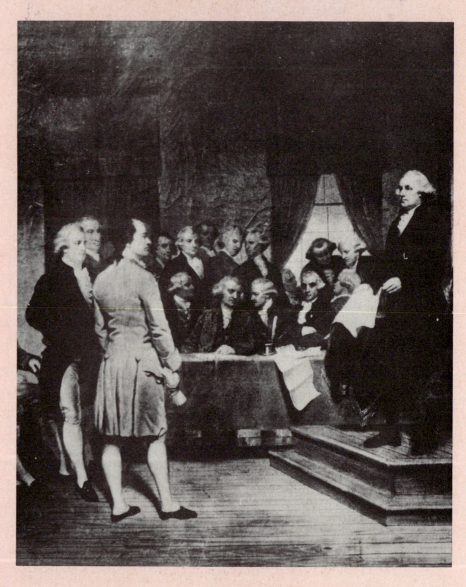

The Constitution was signed in 1787. The Constitution is the supreme law of the United States. All other laws must agree with the Constitution.

Talk It Over

Read and discuss.

The beginning of the Constitution is called the Preamble.
It starts with "We the people . . ."

Dialogues: Practice with a partner.

- S1: What is the Preamble?
- ▶ S2: The Preamble is the first part of the Constitution.

- S1: What does the Constitution say?
- ▶ S2: It says what the government can do.
- S1: What can the government do?
- ▶ S2: The U.S. government has the power to pass laws, collect taxes, print money, and form an army.

Information

 Read the sentences.

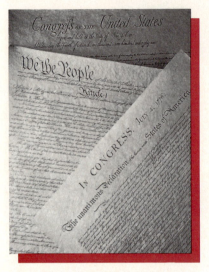

The Bill of Rights is the first ten Amendments, or changes to the Constitution. These are rights that the government cannot take away.

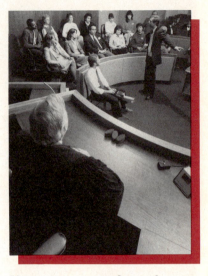

If you are arrested, you have a right to a trial by jury and to a lawyer.

A person has the right *not* to testify against himself or herself in a court of law.

The Bill of Rights also protects against cruel and unusual punishment.

Information

📖 **Read the sentences.**

U.S. Citizens have many new rights. For example, citizens of the U.S. can bring close family members to the United States.

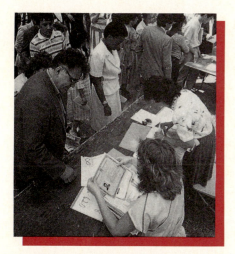

The most important right of citizens is the right to vote. Constitutional Amendments 15, 19, and 26 give the right to vote.

Citizens have a number of other benefits. One benefit is U.S. Citizens can apply for federal government jobs.

Figure It Out

 Complete the puzzle.

Across

1. The beginning of the Constitution is called the _____.

5. The _____ is the supreme law of the United States.

6. A citizen's most important right is the right to _____.

7. Citizens have the right to bring _____ family members to the United States.

Down

2. An _____ is a change.

3. The first ten Amendments to the Constitution are the Bill of _____.

4. The Constitution gives the government _____ to pass laws, collect taxes, print money, and raise an army.

Lesson 5   The Civil War

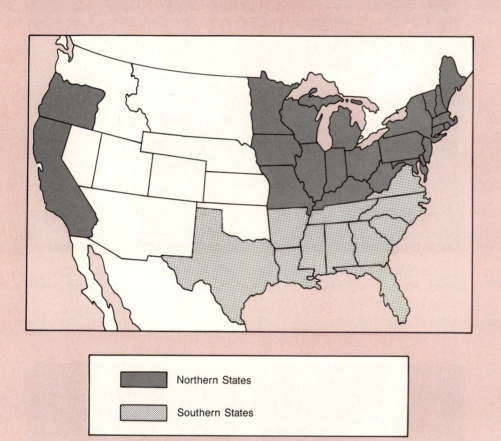

Northern States

Southern States

Americans fought the Civil War from 1861 to 1865. The Southern states wanted to leave the United States and start their own country. They fought against the Northern states.

Information

 Read the sentences.

The Civil War divided the nation in half. The states were no longer *united*. Slavery was one of the causes of the Civil War. The South wanted to maintain slavery. The North wanted to end slavery.

The Southern states were called the Confederacy. Robert E. Lee commanded the Confederate army in the South.

The Northern states were called the Union. Ulysses S. Grant commanded the Union army in the North.

Talk It Over

Lincoln was determined that the nation, and democracy, would *not* be destroyed.

Sojourner Truth was the first black woman to speak out against slavery. In 1864, she visited President Lincoln at the White House.

Dialogues: Practice with a partner.

- S1: Abraham Lincoln was our 16th president.
- S2: Wasn't he President during the Civil War?
- S1: Yes, he was. He signed the Emancipation Proclamation.

- S2: What is the Emancipation Proclamation?
- S1: It's a document that freed the slaves.
- S2: That's right. Abraham Lincoln wanted freedom for everybody.

Figure It Out

Circle the correct answer.

1. The Northern states wanted to maintain slavery. yes no

2. Abraham Lincoln signed the Emancipation Proclamation. yes no

3. The Confederate states were in the South. yes no

4. The Emancipation Proclamation ended slavery. yes no

5. The Union states were in the South. yes no

Complete the puzzle.

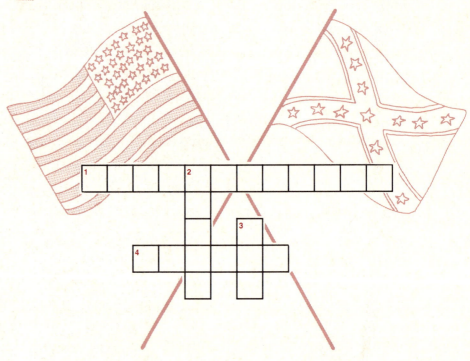

Across

1. The _____ Proclamation declared that the slaves were free.

4. The Civil War divided the nation. The states were no longer _____.

Down

2. Abraham Lincoln was president during the _____ War.

3. Robert E. _____ commanded the Confederate army in the South.

Lesson 6 | World War

In 1914, the nations of Europe went to war and World War I began. The United States entered World War I in 1917. The United States, England, France, and Russia fought against Germany and Austria-Hungary.

Talk It Over

🔺 🔊   **Dialogues: Practice with a partner.**

- S1: What happened after World War I?

▶ S2: Well, the world economy failed. Many people lost their jobs, money, and homes.

- S1: Was that the Great Depression?

▶ S2: Yes, it was.

- S1: During the Great Depression, World War II began.

▶ S2: When did the United States enter World War II?

- S1: In 1941. The United States fought against dictators in Germany, Italy, and Japan.

▶ S2: Which countries were U.S. allies?

- S1: England, France, and Russia.

- S1: The Allies won the war in 1945.

▶ S2: Before the war was over, world leaders met to start the United Nations.

- S1: Right. They wanted to try to stop future wars.

Face to Face

 Read the sentences.

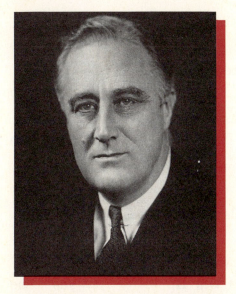

Franklin Roosevelt was President during the Great Depression and World War II.

There were many homeless people during the Great Depression. It was a hard time for many Americans.

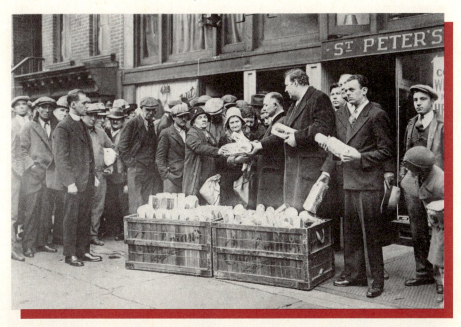

People stood in long lines to get food during the Depression. President Roosevelt tried to help by signing laws that gave people jobs.

Figure It Out

Circle the correct answer.

1. The United States entered World War I in 1941.   yes   no

2. The Great Depression started before World War I.   yes   no

3. Franklin Roosevelt was President during the Depression and World War II.   yes   no

4. During the Great Depression, people lived well.   yes   no

5. Franklin Roosevelt signed laws that gave people jobs.   yes   no

6. Germany, Italy, and Japan were allies of the United States during World War II.   yes   no

7. The United States and its allies won World War II.   yes   no

8. The United Nations tries to help stop wars.   yes   no

Winston Churchill, Franklin Roosevelt, and Joseph Stalin were leaders of the Allies during World War II.

Lesson 7 Vietnam War

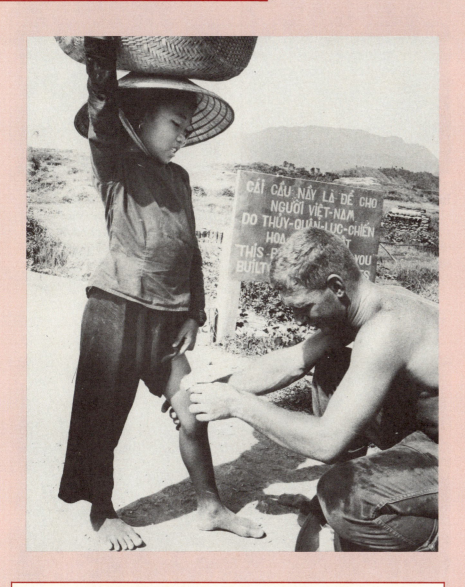

The nation of Vietnam was fighting a civil war. The people of North Vietnam wanted a Communist government. The people of South Vietnam did not want communism. In 1962, the first American soldiers were sent to help South Vietnam.

Information

In 1960, John F. Kennedy was elected president. He was the youngest president in the history of the United States. He sent the first U.S. soldiers to Vietnam.

President Kennedy was assassinated in 1963. Vice President Lyndon Johnson immediately became president. Johnson sent more soldiers to Vietnam.

U.S. citizens did not agree about the Vietnam War. Some wanted the U.S. to leave Vietnam. In 1973, the United States brought all the soldiers home.

Figure It Out

A U.S. helicopter in Vietnam picks up casualties.

The Vietnam Memorial in Washington, D.C., honors the many Americans who died in that war.

Match.

1. The United States went to war to help . . .   Lyndon Johnson.

2. The Communist government was in . . .   South Vietnam.

3. The President who first sent troops to Vietnam was . . .   North Vietnam.

4. President Kennedy was elected in . . .   John F. Kennedy.

5. President Kennedy was assassinated in . . .   1960.

6. The man who became president after Kennedy was assassinated was . . .   1963.

7. The year in which all the American troops were finally brought home from Vietnam was . . .   1973.

Unit 3   U.S. Holidays

Lesson 8 Thanksgiving Day

Americans celebrate Thanksgiving on the fourth Thursday in November. Thanksgiving was the first American holiday. On Thanksgiving Day Americans give thanks for the good things in their lives. They have a special meal and invite their family and friends to join them.

Information

In 1620, a group of people sailed from England in search of religious freedom. The people were Pilgrims. Their sailing ship was called the *Mayflower*.

The Pilgrims suffered during the first winter in America. They had little food. Native Americans helped the Pilgrims plant corn and hunt animals for food. After the first harvest, the Pilgrims and Native Americans shared a large dinner.

Figure It Out

 Complete the puzzle.

The Pilgrims were thankful for their harvest and new home.

Across

2. The _____ helped the Pilgrims.
4. The _____ left England in 1620.
5. The Pilgrims left England for religious _____.

Down

1. After the harvest, they had a large _____.
2. Americans celebrate Thanksgiving in _____.
3. The Pilgrims came to America on the _____.

Lesson 9 Independence Day

The Fourth of July is an American holiday. Celebrations include fireworks, picnics, and parades. Americans remember the signing of the Declaration of Independence on July 4, 1776. July 4th is Independence Day, a day to remember liberty.

Talk It Over

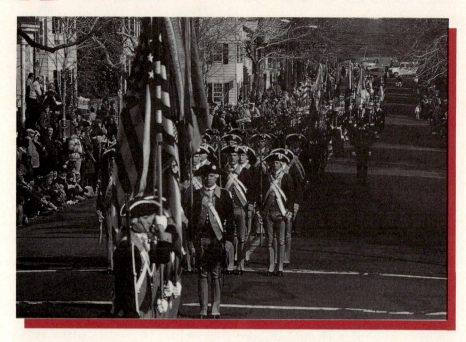

- S1: Why do Americans celebrate July 4th?

▶ S2: Because July 4th is Independence Day.
On July 4, 1776, the thirteen colonies declared their independence.

▶ S2: Who wrote the Declaration of Independence?

• S1: Thomas Jefferson wrote most of the document.

▶ S2: How many people signed it?

• S1: Fifty-six, including Thomas Jefferson, Benjamin Franklin, and John Adams.

• S1: So, July 4th celebrates the beginning of the United States?

▶ S2: Exactly. July 4th is America's birthday.

Extension

 Read the sentences.

Francis Scott Key wrote "The Star-Spangled Banner" in 1814. He ended the song with these words:
"Oh! say, does that star-spangled banner yet wave
O'er the land of the free and the home of the brave?"

The American flag is a symbol of the United States. "The Star-Spangled Banner" was written in honor of the flag. The song is America's national anthem.

Many brave Americans have given their lives to keep the United States a free nation.

Figure It Out

 Complete the puzzle.

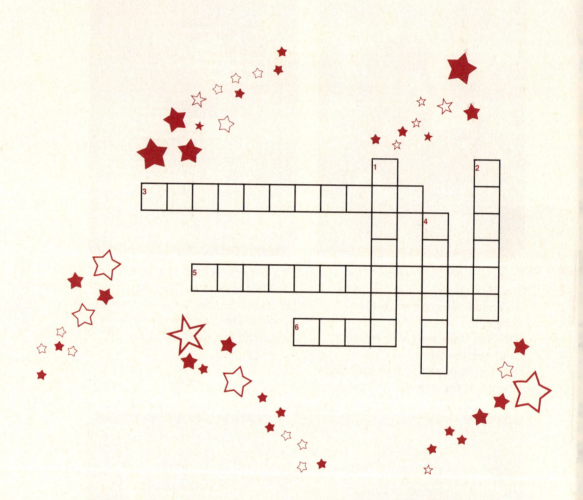

	Across		Down

Across

3. Americans remember the signing of the _____ of Independence on July 4th.
5. Thomas Jefferson wrote most of the Declaration of _____.
6. _____ 4th is Independence Day.

Down

1. The Fourth of July is an American _____.
2. "The Star-Spangled Banner" is America's national _____.
4. "The Star-Spangled _____" was written in honor of the U.S. flag.

Lesson 10 Other Holidays

Most Americans get time off from work to remember special people or events in American history. These holidays include Memorial Day and Labor Day.

Face to Face

 Read the sentences.

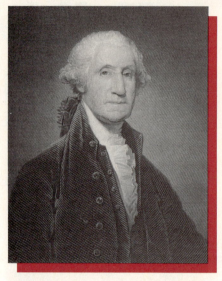

Presidents' Day is a holiday to remember George Washington and Abraham Lincoln. We remember George Washington as the "Father of Our Country."

We remember Abraham Lincoln for signing the Emancipation Proclamation. Presidents' Day is the third Monday in February.

Martin Luther King, Jr., is remembered on the third Monday in January.

We remember him as a civil rights leader. He helped Black Americans obtain the rights guaranteed to them in the Constitution.

Copy It Down

Write the sentences.

1. Memorial Day became a holiday after World War I.

_____

_____

2. On Memorial Day Americans remember those
   individuals who died in war.

_____

_____

_____

3. Memorial Day is the last Monday in May.

_____

_____

4. Veterans Day also started after World War I.

_____

_____

5. On November 11 we honor all Americans who have
   served in the armed forces.

_____

_____

_____

Information

 Read the sentences.

Labor Day is the first Monday in September. We honor all the workers in America on that day.

Columbus Day is the second Monday in October. We remember Christopher Columbus, who arrived in the Americas in 1492. Columbus claimed the land for Spain.

Figure It Out

Circle the dates of these holidays on the calendars below.

Labor Day	Martin Luther King, Jr., Day
Veterans Day	Columbus Day
Presidents' Day	Memorial Day

JANUARY

SUN	MON	TUES	WED	THU	FRI	SAT
1	2	3	4	5	6	7
8	9	10	11	12	13	14
15	16	17	18	19	20	21
22	23	24	25	26	27	28
29	30	31				

FEBRUARY

SUN	MON	TUES	WED	THU	FRI	SAT
		1	2	3	4	
5	6	7	8	9	10	11
12	13	14	15	16	17	18
19	20	21	22	23	24	25
26	27	28				

MAY

SUN	MON	TUES	WED	THU	FRI	SAT
	1	2	3	4	5	6
7	8	9	10	11	12	13
14	15	16	17	18	19	20
21	22	23	24	25	26	27
28	29	30	31			

SEPTEMBER

SUN	MON	TUES	WED	THU	FRI	SAT
					1	2
3	4	5	6	7	8	9
10	11	12	13	14	15	16
17	18	19	20	21	22	23
24	25	26	27	28	29	30

OCTOBER

SUN	MON	TUES	WED	THU	FRI	SAT
1	2	3	4	5	6	7
8	9	10	11	12	13	14
15	16	17	18	19	20	21
22	23	24	25	26	27	28
29	30	31				

NOVEMBER

SUN	MON	TUES	WED	THU	FRI	SAT
		1	2	3	4	
5	6	7	8	9	10	11
12	13	14	15	16	17	18
19	20	21	22	23	24	25
26	27	28	29	30		

Unit 4 | U.S. Government

Lesson 11 Legislative Branch

The Constitution set up the U.S. government in three branches. One branch is the legislative branch. The legislative branch makes laws.

Information

 Read the sentences.

Congress makes the laws of the nation. The Congress is made up of two different groups of lawmakers—the Senate and the House of Representatives.

Both the Senate and the House of Representatives meet in the Capitol Building. The Capitol Building is in Washington, D.C.

Copy It Down

Write the information.

1. Congress is the legislative branch of the government.

   _____

   _____

2. The House of Representatives and the Senate form the Congress.

   _____

   _____

THE CONGRESS	
House of Representatives	**Senate**
_____ representative for a certain number of people = _____ representatives	_____ senators from each state = _____ Senators
Elected every _____ years	Elected every _____ years
Can be elected any number of times	Can be elected any number of times
Must be a citizen—either born in the U.S. or naturalized	Must be a citizen—either born in the U.S. or naturalized
Must be at least _____ years old	Must be at least _____ years old

Talk It Over

- S1: How are the members of Congress chosen?
- S2: Citizens vote for them.
- S1: You mean that representatives and senators are elected by the people?
- S2: That's right.

- S1: What does Congress do?
- S2: Congress passes laws.
- S1: What kind of laws?
- S2: Laws about taxes and trade.
- S1: Can Congress declare war?
- S2: Yes, it can.

Figure It Out

 Write short answers to the questions.

1. What is the legislative branch of the government called?

_____

2. What are the two parts of Congress?

_____

3. Who elects the members of Congress?

_____

4. How many senators are in Congress?

_____

5. How many representatives are in Congress?

_____

6. How long is the term of a representative?

_____

7. How long is the term of a senator?

_____

Lesson 12 Executive Branch

The President is head of the executive branch of the U.S. government. The President is chief executive. The executive branch enforces the law.

Information

 Read the sentences.

The President lives and works in the White House. The President is Commander in Chief of the armed services. The President signs bills into law.

The Vice President is elected with the President. If the President dies, the Vice President becomes President. The main duty of the Vice President is to preside over the Senate.

The Cabinet is also part of the executive branch. The Cabinet helps the President enforce the law. The President chooses the members of the Cabinet. The Senate approves them.

Talk It Over

Dialogues: Practice with a partner.

● S1: How often is the President elected?

► S2: Every four years.

● S1: How long can the President serve?

► S2: Two terms, or eight years.

● S1: When is the next presidential election?

► S2: In November 1996.

● S1: When is the President inaugurated?

► S2: Two months later, in January.

● S1: What are the requirements to be President?

► S2: The President must be at least 35 years old and must be a citizen born in the United States.

Figure It Out

Write the letter of the person responsible for each duty.

A. President	B. Vice President

_____ 1. Becomes president if the President dies

_____ 2. Is the Commander in Chief of the armed services

_____ 3. Heads the executive branch of the government

_____ 4. Presides over the Senate

_____ 5. Lives and works in the White House

Circle the correct words.

1. The President's term is _____ years.

   eight　　　four　　　six

2. The President may be re-elected _____.

   one time　　　four times　　　three times

3. The President must be at least _____ years old.

   45　　　40　　　35

4. The President must be a citizen _____ in the United States.

   naturalized　　　born　　　imprisoned

5. The election for President is held in _____.

   November　　　January　　　December

6. The inauguration is held in _____.

   November　　　January　　　December

Lesson 13 Judicial Branch

The Supreme Court is the third branch of the U.S. government. The nine Supreme Court judges interpret the law. They make sure laws agree with the Constitution. Another word for judge is *justice*.

Talk It Over

■ ■ **Dialogues: Practice with a partner.**

- ● S1: The judges, or justices, hear cases brought by the people.

- ▶ S2: Is the Supreme Court the only court of law?

- ● S1: No, there are city, state, and federal courts.

- ▶ S2: But the Supreme Court is the highest in the land?

- ● S1: That's right. Its decisions are final.

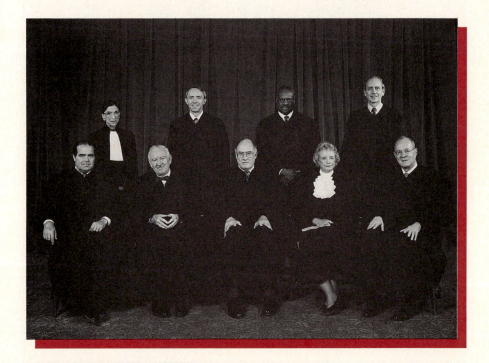

- ● S1: What if the justices don't agree?

- ▶ S2: They take a vote, and the majority rules.

- ● S1: Can the President fire a justice?

- ▶ S2: No, the justices serve for as long as they are able.

Copy It Down

✍ **Write the sentences.**

1. The Supreme Court is the highest court in the judicial branch.

_____

_____

2. The justices decide if the laws agree with the Constitution.

_____

_____

3. When the judges are deciding a case, the Chief Justice leads the discussion.

_____

_____

_____

4. The decisions of the Supreme Court are final.

_____

_____

Figure It Out

Read the information in the boxes. Write the letter of the box under the building the information matches.

A. **Executive branch**

Enforces the laws
The President is head of the executive
   branch.

B. **Legislative branch**

Makes the laws
The Congress is made up of the Senate
   and the House of Representatives.

C. **Judicial branch**

Interprets the laws
The highest court in the nation is the
   Supreme Court.

Lesson 14 States and Capitals

Each state in the United States has its own government. Each state government can make its own rules and laws. But these laws must agree with the U.S. Constitution.

Information

 Read and discuss.

The capital city in each state is the seat of government. Here the state laws are made for each state.

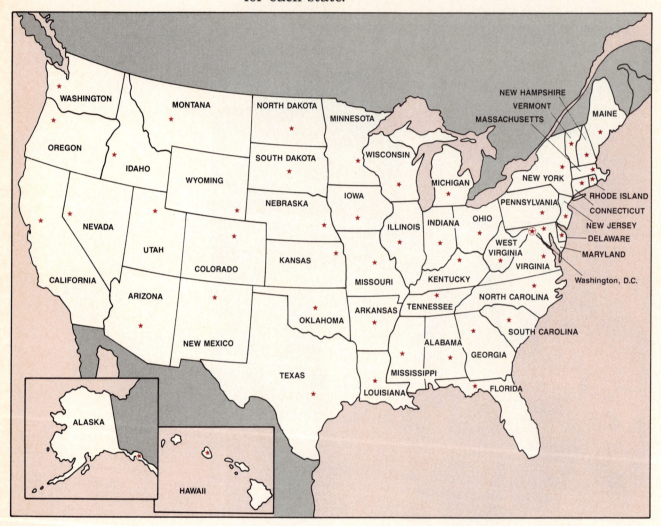

Map Key

State (state abbreviations)	★ State Capital
Alaska (AK)	★ Juneau
Alabama (AL)	★ Montgomery
Arkansas (AR)	★ Little Rock
Arizona (AZ)	★ Phoenix
California (CA)	★ Sacramento
Colorado (CO)	★ Denver
Connecticut (CT)	★ Hartford
Delaware (DE)	★ Dover
Florida (FL)	★ Tallahassee
Georgia (GA)	★ Atlanta
Hawaii (HI)	★ Honolulu
Iowa (IA)	★ Des Moines
Idaho (ID)	★ Boise
Illinois (IL)	★ Springfield
Indiana (IN)	★ Indianapolis

Kansas (KS)	★ Topeka
Kentucky (KY)	★ Frankfort
Louisiana (LA)	★ Baton Rouge
Massachusetts (MA)	★ Boston
Maryland (MD)	★ Annapolis
Maine (ME)	★ Augusta
Michigan (MI)	★ Lansing
Minnesota (MN)	★ St. Paul
Missouri (MO)	★ Jefferson City
Mississippi (MS)	★ Jackson
Montana (MT)	★ Helena
North Carolina (NC)	★ Raleigh
North Dakota (ND)	★ Bismark
Nebraska (NE)	★ Lincoln
New Hampshire (NH)	★ Concord
New Jersey (NJ)	★ Trenton
New Mexico (NM)	★ Santa Fe
Nevada (NV)	★ Carson City

New York (NY)	★ Albany
Ohio (OH)	★ Columbus
Oklahoma (OK)	★ Oklahoma City
Oregon (OR)	★ Salem
Pennsylvania (PA)	★ Harrisburg
Rhode Island (RI)	★ Providence
South Carolina (SC)	★ Columbia
South Dakota (SD)	★ Pierre
Tennessee (TN)	★ Nashville
Texas (TX)	★ Austin
Utah (UT)	★ Salt Lake City
Virginia (VA)	★ Richmond
Vermont (VT)	★ Montpelier
Washington (WA)	★ Olympia
Wisconsin (WI)	★ Madison
West Virginia (WV)	★ Charleston
Wyoming (WY)	★ Cheyenne

Talk It Over

 Dialogues: Practice with a partner.

- S1: Where are you from?
- ► S2: I'm from _____, but now I live in the United States.
- S1: What state do you live in?
- ► S2: I live in _____.
- S1: What is the capital of your state?
- ► S2: _____ is the capital.

- S1: Find Florida on the map. What's the capital?
- ► S2: Tallahassee.
- S1: Austin is the capital of which state?
- ► S2: Texas.
- S1: What about the capital of California?
- ► S2: Sacramento.
- S1: Very good!
- ► S2: Thank you.

Copy It Down

 **Write the sentences.**

1. States pass their own laws on education, taxes, roads,
   and marriage.

   _____

   _____

2. The people elect state legislators to make state laws.

   _____

   _____

3. The head of each state is the governor. The governor
   enforces the laws.

   _____

   _____

4. Judges in state courts interpret state laws.

   _____

   _____

Figure It Out

 Imagine that you are planning a trip to visit several state capitals. Below is the map of your trip. Look at the map on page 66 to find the names of the cities and states you'll be visiting. Write the names on the lines below.

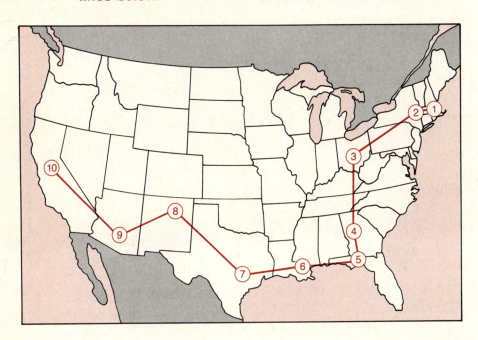

	State	Capital
1.	_____	_____
2.	_____	_____
3.	_____	_____
4.	_____	_____
5.	_____	_____
6.	_____	_____
7.	_____	_____
8.	_____	_____
9.	_____	_____
10.	_____	_____

Lesson 15   U.S. Political System

The United States is a republic. In this form of government the people elect their leaders. Two main political parties in the U.S. compete for those votes. These are the Republican and Democratic parties.

Information

 Read the sentences.

Republicans and Democrats have similar goals. Both of these political parties want to protect the country and work for its welfare. But the two parties have different ways of achieving these goals.

The Democrats and Republicans have large meetings called *conventions* every four years. The purpose of these political conventions is to decide on their leaders and policies.

Copy It Down

 City, state, and federal governments have three branches. Fill in the chart with the names of the people who hold those offices today, including state and city officials in your area.

FEDERAL		
Executive Branch	**Legislative Branch**	**Judicial Branch**
President: _____	Senators: _____ _____	Chief Justice: _____
Vice President: _____	Representative: _____	
Party: _____		

STATE		
Executive Branch	**Legislative Branch**	**Judicial Branch**
Governor: _____	State Senators: _____ _____	Chief Justice: _____
Party: _____	Representative: _____	

CITY		
Executive Branch	**Legislative Branch**	**Judicial Branch**
Mayor or City manager: _____	City council	Municipal courts

Figure It Out

Write the correct words from the box.

Democrats	donkey	republic
mayor	protect	elephant

1. The United States form of government is a

   _____.

2. Republicans and _____ belong to the
   two main political parties in the U.S.

3. The chief executive of a city government is either a city

   manager or a _____.

4. The symbol of the Republican Party is an

   _____.

5. The symbol of the Democratic Party is a

   _____.

6. One goal of the Republicans and Democrats is to

   _____ the country.

APPENDIX

U.S. History Time Line

1787 Constitution signed

1620 Pilgrims land at Plymouth, Massachusetts

1776 Declaration of Independence signed

1600   1700   1800

1775 Revolutionary War starts

1783 Revolutionary War ends

1788 George Washington elected first president

1863 Lincoln signs Emancipation Proclamation

1929 Great Depression begins

1964 Civil Rights Law passed

1800 Thomas Jefferson elected president

1886 Statue of Liberty erected

1800

1900

2000

1814 "Star-Spangled Banner" written

1865 Civil war ends

1914–1918 World War I

1861 Civil war begins

1939–1945 World War II

1957–1975 Vietnam War

APPENDIX

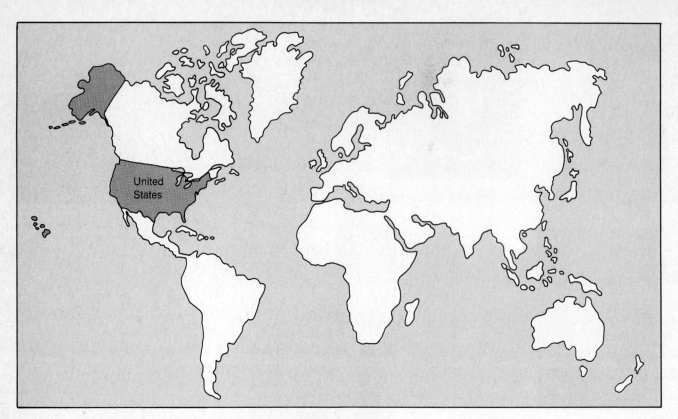

The World

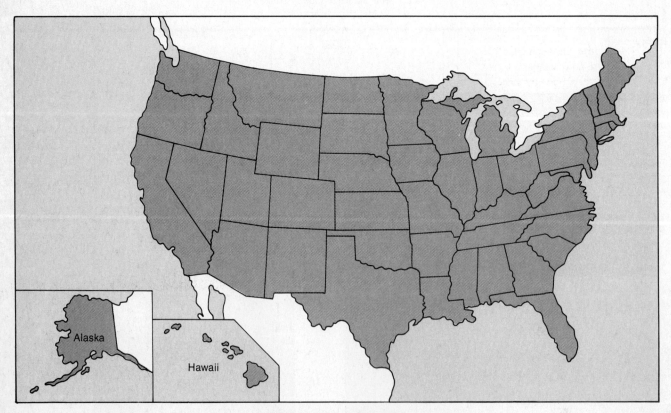

The United States

Preparation for Citizenship

Instructor's Section

Contents

Scope and Sequence

UNIT 1: U.S. SYMBOLS

Lesson 1:   The Flag
Lesson 2:   Pledge of Allegiance

UNIT 2: U.S. HISTORY

Lesson 3:   The Revolutionary War
(Declaration of Independence,
Liberty Bell)
Lesson 4:   The Constitution
(Bill of Rights, Citizenship)
Lesson 5:   The Civil War
(Abraham Lincoln,
Emancipation Proclamation,
Lincoln Memorial)
Lesson 6:   World War
(World War I, The Great
Depression, Franklin Delano
Roosevelt, World War II)
Lesson 7:   Vietnam
(John F. Kennedy)

UNIT 3: U.S. HOLIDAYS

Lesson 8:   Thanksgiving
(Native Americans)
Lesson 9:   Independence Day
(National Anthem)
Lesson 10:   Other Holidays (Presidents' Day,
Martin Luther King, Jr., Day,
Memorial Day, Veteran's Day,
Labor Day, Columbus Day)

UNIT 4: U.S. GOVERNMENT

Lesson 11:   Legislative Branch
Lesson 12:   Executive Branch
Lesson 13:   Judicial Branch
Lesson 14:   States and Capitals
(City, State, and National Law)
Lesson 15:   The U.S. Political System
(Two-party system, Current office
holders)

APPENDIX

Introduction

The purpose of *Preparation for Citizenship* is to help learners prepare for U.S. citizenship. This program mirrors instructional requirements set forth by the U.S. Immigration and Naturalization Service (INS). *Preparation for Citizenship* addresses the basic language skills of listening, speaking, reading, and writing, as well as emphasizing vocabulary development. A maximum number of photos and illustrations are used throughout the series. These graphics serve as springboards for classroom discussion and also serve to ease the student's way through some of the more difficult concepts inherent in the study of citizenship.

The information in this section describes how to best utilize this Worktext®. While it may be helpful to the students, it is intended for the instructor's use.

This section also provides 100 Citizenship Study Questions, with answers shown in brackets. Included also are a variety of Blackline Masters. These Blackline Masters provide additional information such as the Star-Spangled Banner, the Bill of Rights, and practice pages for filling out personal forms.

Organization of the Student's Book

This Worktext® features four consistently organized units: U.S. Symbols, U.S. History, U.S. Holidays, and U.S. Government. Each unit is divided into a varying number of lessons. The lessons contain activity pages that focus on the following skills: listening, speaking, reading, writing, and problem solving. These activity pages are listed below.

Talk It Over

In these sections, dialogues provide oral practice. The dialogues link additional information to previously presented material. Initially, each dialogue may be conducted as a whole-class exercise. Model the dialogue as students follow along in their books. You may then want to divide the class in half, with one side reading the part of Student 1 (S1) while the other reads Student 2 (S2). Reverse the parts until both groups can read the dialogue smoothly. As students become more confident and comfortable working in groups, encourage pair work.

Information

The Information sections provide additional facts and contain photos that are intended to stimulate conversation. These sections also contain sentences for learners to read. Occasionally these sentences take the form of a dialogue. Information pages give learners an opportunity to read aloud and to discuss relevant facts in an interesting and meaningful context.

Face to Face

These sections present information about important people in history. Visuals support the text. Often dialogues reinforce the text, as well.

Copy It Down

The activities in Copy It Down give learners an opportunity to practice writing in English. These pages offer clear models for students to follow. Single words are written first. These are then combined into phrases and/or sentences. The sentences offer learners another opportunity to read aloud, reinforcing the facts being presented.

Extension

An Extension page provides extended and related information on the lesson topic. These pages also provide practice in basic language skills of listening, reading, and writing, as well as vocabulary development.

Figure It Out

The exercises on the Figure It Out page reinforce the lesson material and provide practice in writing. Initially, the exercises are best presented as whole-class activities. Each student marks his or her paper as the teacher models the activity on the chalkboard. When students become familiar with the various formats, they may work in groups, pairs, or individually.

Communication Strategies

Getting Students Involved

Take advantage of what students already know. Before introducing a new lesson, ask students what they know about the subject. Adult learners have a wealth of information and experience to bring to the learning process. Successfully activating this background information will have a decisive impact on their ability to make sense of what they read, hear, and understand. Intercultural communication —soliciting information about the student's life experiences in his or her native culture—is an important strategy in any ESL classroom. Comparing and contrasting the history, government, culture, and customs of the United States with those of the student's native country may open valuable doors of communication and student involvement.

Working in Groups

Give students a chance to learn from each other. Have students work in groups or with partners to give them an opportunity to help each other and to use the language in a natural context. Encouraging students to interact in English will help reinforce concepts and vocabulary and will extend students' productive use of the language.

Teaching Procedures

Building Vocabulary

Follow these steps for introducing new vocabulary words.

1. Write the target word, such as NAME, on the board in uppercase (capital) letters.
2. Pronounce the word syllable by syllable. Have learners repeat it several times in this manner. Then pronounce the word in its entirety and have learners repeat it. Pay careful attention to correct syllabic stress.
3. Define the word. Ask students to use the word in a sentence and/or write the definition in their notebooks.

Grammar Check

Every page of text may be used to practice and reinforce grammatical structures. For example, when presenting the sentence "The flag has stars and stripes," one could practice singular and plural agreement. Consider the number of variations suitable for drill and practice:

"The flags have stars and stripes."
"I have a flag."
"Manuel has a flag."
"She has a flag."

Whenever possible, explore as many avenues of grammar as a single utterance can provide. "The flag has stars and stripes," for example, may also be used as a springboard for practice with question and answer formation:

"Does the flag have stars and stripes?" ("Yes, it does.")
"Does Manuel have a flag?" ("Yes, he does." or "No, he doesn't.")

Below are examples of other sentences that could be used for grammar practice:

Tense: "George Washington *was* our first president."
"Bill Clinton *is* President today."

Negative Formation: "The colonists *wanted* freedom."
"The colonists *did not want* to pay high taxes."

Contractions: "*Where's* the Jefferson Memorial?"
"*Where is* the Jefferson Memorial?"

Possessives: "Congress makes the *country's laws.*"
"Congress makes the *laws of our country.*"
"The *President's office* is in the White House."
"The *office of the President* is in the White House."

Context Clues

Teach students to rely on context as much as possible in understanding unknown words. When a student encounters an unfamiliar word in text, employ a questioning technique:

1. What word would make sense here?
2. Put your finger over the word and go back to the beginning of the sentence. What word would make sense in this sentence?
3. If students do not suggest a word, cover the end of the word. Point to the beginning of the word and ask if they can think of a word that begins like that and that would make sense.
4. If the students still cannot read the word in context, model the word for the students and have them read the sentence again.

Cloze Practice

Choose a passage students already have read. Leave the first and last sentences or phrases intact. Beginning with the second sentence, black out every fifth word, leaving only the first letter. Have students take turns providing a word to fill in the blank. First perform the activity as a whole class exercise, with students taking turns guessing at the word and reading the passage. Later, use the activity as a group or individual exercise with students taking turns and comparing answers. Include some follow-up questions to check comprehension and always compare the students' version with the original.

Word Map

In this exercise, an abstract concept such as GOVERNMENT is made more concrete by demonstrating its relationships. A word map concerned with the concept of GOVERNMENT may look something like this:

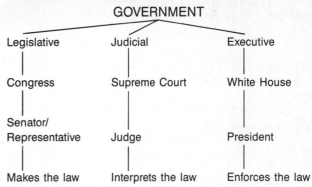

Below is a different word map concerned with the concept of LAW.

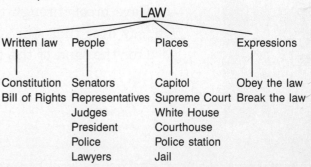

Star-Spangled Banner

Oh, say can you see by the dawn's early light
   What so proudly we hailed at the twilight's last gleaming?
Whose broad stripes and bright stars thru the perilous fight,
   O'er the ramparts we watched were so gallantly streaming?
And the rocket's red glare, the bombs bursting in air,
   Gave proof through the night that our flag was still there.
Oh, say does that star-spangled banner yet wave
   O'er the land of the free and the home of the brave?

Bill of Rights

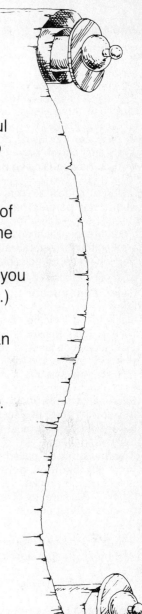

1. Freedom of religion. (You can go to any church you want to . . . or no church at all.)

   Freedom of speech. (You can say or write whatever you believe to be true.)

   Right to petition and assemble. (You can join in peaceful meetings and protests. You can ask the government to correct wrongs.)

2. Right to "keep and bear (fire)arms."

3. Freedom to decide who lives in your home in times of peace. Soldiers cannot be assigned to a private home without the owner's consent—except in wartime.

4. Freedom from unlawful search. (No one can search you or your belongings without a legal permit, or warrant.)

5. Right to a grand jury in case of serious crime.

   Right to refuse to testify against yourself. (No one can make you say things that will get you in trouble with the law.)

   Protection against being tried twice for the same crime. (If you are found "not guilty" in a trial, you cannot be accused and tried again for the same crime.)

6. Right to a fair trial by jury in criminal cases.

   Right to a lawyer.

7. Right to a fair trial by jury in most civil cases.

8. Right to reasonable bails, fines, and punishments. (*Bail* is money given to the court when an accused person is released before his/her trial takes place.)

9. Protection of rights not named in the Constitution.

10. Protection of the powers of individual states.

INSTRUCTIONS

Purpose of This Form.
This form is for use to apply to become a naturalized citizen of the United States.

Who May File.
You may apply for naturalization if:
- you have been a lawful permanent resident for five years;
- you have been a lawful permanent resident for three years, have been married to a United States citizen for those three years, and continue to be married to that U.S. citizen;
- you are the lawful permanent resident child of United States citizen parents; or
- you have qualifying military service.

Children under 18 may automatically become citizens when their parents naturalize. You may inquire at your local Service office for further information. If you do not meet the qualifications listed above but believe that you are eligible for naturalization, you may inquire at your local Service office for additional information.

General Instructions.
Please answer all questions by typing or clearly printing in black ink. Indicate that an item is not applicable with "N/A". If an answer is "none," write "none". If you need extra space to answer any item, attach a sheet of paper with your name and your alien registration number (A#), if any, and indicate the number of the item.

Every application must be properly signed and filed with the correct fee. If you are under 18 years of age, your parent or guardian must sign the application.

If you wish to be called for your examination at the same time as another person who is also applying for naturalization, make your request on a separate cover sheet. Be sure to give the name and alien registration number of that person.

Initial Evidence Requirements.
You must file your application with the following evidence:

A copy of your alien registration card.

Photographs. You must submit two color photographs of yourself taken within 30 days of this application. These photos must be glossy, unretouched and unmounted, and have a white background. Dimension of the face should be about 1 inch from chin to top of hair. Face should be 3/4 frontal view of right side with right ear visible. Using pencil or felt pen, lightly print name and A#, if any, on the back of each photo. This requirement may be waived by the Service if you can establish that you are confined because of age or physical infirmity.

Fingerprints. If you are between the ages of 14 and 75, you must sumit your fingerprints on Form FD-258. Fill out the form and write your Alien Registration Number in the space marked "Your No. OCA" or "Miscellaneous No. MNU". Take the chart and these instructions to a police station, sheriff's office or an office of this Service, or other reputable person or organization for fingerprinting. (You should contact the police or sheriff's office before going there since some of these offices do not take fingerprints for other government agencies.) You must sign the chart in the presence of the person taking your fingerprints and have that person sign his/her name, title, and the date in the space provided. Do not bend, fold, or crease the fingerprint chart.

U.S. Military Service. If you have ever served in the Armed Forces of the United States at any time, you must submit a completed Form G-325B. If your application is based on your military service you must also submit Form N-426, "Request for Certification of Military or Naval Service."

Application for Child. If this application is for a permanent resident child of U.S. citizen parents, you must also submit copies of the child's birth certificate, the parents' marriage certificate, and evidence of the parents' U.S. citizenship. If the parents are divorced, you must also submit the divorce decree and evidence that the citizen parent has legal custody of the child.

Where to File.
File this application at the local Service office having jurisdiction over your place of residence.

Fee.
The fee for this application is $95.00. The fee must be submitted in the exact amount. It cannot be refunded. DO NOT MAIL CASH.

All checks and money orders must be drawn on a bank or other institution located in the United States and must be payable in United States currency. The check or money order should be made payable to the Immigration and Naturalization Service, except that:
- If you live in Guam, and are filing this application in Guam, make your check or money order payable to the "Treasurer, Guam."
- If you live in the Virgin Islands, and are filing this application in the Virgin Islands, make your check or money order payable to the "Commissioner of Finance of the Virgin Islands."

Checks are accepted subject to collection. An uncollected check will render the application and any document issued invalid. A charge of $5.00 will be imposed if a check in payment of a fee is not honored by the bank on which it is drawn.

Form N-400 (Rev. 07/17/91) N

Processing Information.

Rejection. Any application that is not signed or is not accompanied by the proper fee will be rejected with a notice that the application is deficient. You may correct the deficiency and resubmit the application. However, an application is not considered properly filed until it is accepted by the Service.

Requests for more information. We may request more information or evidence. We may also request that you submit the originals of any copy. We will return these originals when they are no longer required.

Interview. After you file your application, you will be notified to appear at a Service office to be examined under oath or affirmation. This interview may not be waived. If you are an adult, you must show that you have a knowledge and understanding of the history, principles, and form of government of the United States. There is no exemption from this requirement.

You will also be examined on your ability to read, write, and speak English. If on the date of your examination you are more than 50 years of age and have been a lawful permanent resident for 20 years or more, or you are 55 years of age and have been a lawful permanent resident for at least 15 years, you will be exempt from the English language requirements of the law. If you are exempt, you may take the examination in any language you wish.

Oath of Allegiance. If your application is approved, you will be required to take the following oath of allegiance to the United States in order to become a citizen:

"I hereby declare, on oath, that I absolutely and entirely renounce and abjure all allegiance and fidelity to any foreign prince, potentate, state or sovereignty, of whom or which I have heretofore been a subject or citizen; that I will support and defend the Constitution and laws of the United States of America against all enemies, foreign and domestic; that I will bear true faith and allegiance to the same; that I will bear arms on behalf of the United States when required by the law; that I will perform noncombatant service in the armed forces of the United States when required by the law; that I will perform work of national importance under civilian direction when required by the law; and that I take this obligation freely without any mental reservation or purpose of evasion; so help me God."

If you cannot promise to bear arms or perform noncombatant service because of religious training and belief, you may omit those statements when taking the oath. "Religious training and belief" means a person's belief in relation to a Supreme Being involving duties superior to those arising from any human relation, but does not include essentially political, sociological, or philosophical views or merely a personal moral code.

Oath ceremony. You may choose to have the oath of allegiance administered in a ceremony conducted by the Service or request to be scheduled for an oath ceremony in a court that has jurisdiction over the applicant's place of residence. At the time of your examination you will be asked to elect either form of ceremony. You will become a citizen on the date of the oath ceremony and the Attorney General will issue a Certificate of Naturalization as evidence of United States citizenship.

If you wish to change your name as part of the naturalization process, you will have to take the oath in court.

Penalties.

If you knowingly and willfully falsify or conceal a material fact or submit a false document with this request, we will deny the benefit you are filing for, and may deny any other immigration benefit. In addition, you will face severe penalties provided by law, and may be subject to criminal prosecution.

Privacy Act Notice.

We ask for the information on this form, and associated evidence, to determine if you have established eligibility for the immigration benefit you are filing for. Our legal right to ask for this information is in 8 USC 1439, 1440, 1443, 1445, 1446, and 1452. We may provide this information to other government agencies. Failure to provide this information, and any requested evidence, may delay a final decision or result in denial of your request.

Paperwork Reduction Act Notice.

We try to create forms and instructions that are accurate, can be easily understood, and which impose the least possible burden on you to provide us with information. Often this is difficult because some immigration laws are very complex. Accordingly, the reporting burden for this collection of information is computed as follows: (1) learning about the law and form, 20 minutes; (2) completing the form, 25 minutes; and (3) assembling and filing the application (includes statutory required interview and travel time, after filing of application), 3 hours and 35 minutes, for an estimated average of 4 hours and 20 minutes per response. If you have comments regarding the accuracy of this estimate, or suggestions for making this form simpler, you can write to both the Immigration and Naturalization Service, 425 I Street, N.W., Room 5304, Washington, D.C. 20536; and the Office of Management and Budget, Paperwork Reduction Project, OMB No. 1115-0009, Washington, D.C. 20503.

U.S. Department of Justice
Immigration and Naturalization Service

OMB #1115-0009

Application for Naturalization

START HERE - Please Type or Print

Part 1. Information about you.

Family Name	Given Name	Middle Initial

U.S. Mailing Address - Care of

Street Number and Name	Apt. #

City	County

State	ZIP Code

Date of Birth (month/day/year)	Country of Birth

Social Security #	A #

Part 2. Basis for Eligibility (check one).

a. ☐ I have been a permanent resident for at least five (5) years .

b. ☐ I have been a permanent resident for at least three (3) years and have been married to a United States Citizen for those three years.

c. ☐ I am a permanent resident child of United States citizen parent(s) .

d. ☐ I am applying on the basis of qualifying military service in the Armed Forces of the U.S. and have attached completed Forms N-426 and G-325B

e. ☐ Other. (Please specify section of law) _____

Part 3. Additional information about you.

Date you became a permanent resident (month/day/year)	Port admitted with an immmigrant visa or INS Office where granted adjustment of status.

Citizenship

Name on alien registration card (if different than in Part 1)

Other names used since you became a permanent resident (including maiden name)

Sex ☐ Male ☐ Female	Height	Marital Status: ☐ Single ☐ Married	☐ Divorced ☐ Widowed

Can you speak, read and write English ?   ☐No ☐Yes.

Absences from the U.S.:

Have you been absent from the U.S. since becoming a permanent resident?   ☐ No ☐Yes.

If you answered **"Yes"** , complete the following, Begin with your most recent absence. If you need more room to explain the reason for an absence or to list more trips, continue on separate paper.

Date left U.S.	Date returned	Did absence last 6 months or more?	Destination	Reason for trip
		☐ Yes ☐ No		
		☐ Yes ☐ No		
		☐ Yes ☐ No		
		☐ Yes ☐ No		
		☐ Yes ☐ No		
		☐ Yes ☐ No		

Form N-400 (Rev. 07/17/91)N

FOR INS USE ONLY

Returned	Receipt

Resubmitted

Reloc Sent

Reloc Rec'd

☐ Applicant Interviewed

At interview

☐ request naturalization ceremony at court

Remarks

Action

To Be Completed by
Attorney or Representative, if any
☐ Fill in box if G-28 is attached to represent the applicant

VOLAG#

ATTY State License #

Part 4. Information about your residences and employment.

A. List your addresses during the last five (5) years or since you became a permanent resident, whichever is less. Begin with your current address. If you need more space, continue on separate paper:

Street Number and Name, City, State, Country, and Zip Code	Dates (month/day/year)	
	From	To

B. List your employers during the last five (5) years. List your present or most recent employer first. If none, write "None". If you need more space, continue on separate paper.

Employer's Name	Employer's Address	Dates Employed (month/day/year)		Occupation/position
	Street Name and Number - City, State and ZIP Code	From	To	

Part 5. Information about your marital history.

A. Total number of times you have been married _____ . If you are now married, complete the following regarding your husband or wife.

Family name	Given name	Middle initial

Address

Date of birth (month/day/year)	Country of birth	Citizenship
Social Security#	A# (if applicable)	Immigration status (If not a U.S. citizen)

Naturalization (If applicable)
(month/day/year)   Place   (City, State)

If you have ever previously been married or if your current spouse has been previously married, please provide the following on separate paper: Name of prior spouse, date of marriage, date marriage ended, how marriage ended and immigration status of prior spouse.

Part 6. Information about your children.

B. Total Number of Children _____ Complete the following information for each of your children. If the child lives with you, state "with me" in the address column; otherwise give city/state/country of child's current residence. If deceased, write "deceased" in the address column. If you need more space, continue on separate paper.

Full name of child	Date of birth	Country of birth	Citizenship	A - Number	Address

Form N-400 (Rev 07/17/91)N

Part 7. Additional eligibility factors.

Please answer each of the following questions. If your answer is **"Yes"**, explain on a separate paper.

1. Are you now, or have you ever been a member of, or in any way connected or associated with the Communist Party, or ever knowingly aided or supported the Communist Party directly, or indirectly through another organization, group or person, or ever advocated, taught, believed in, or knowingly supported or furthered the interests of communism? ☐ Yes ☐ No

2. During the period March 23, 1933 to May 8, 1945, did you serve in, or were you in any way affiliated with, either directly or indirectly, any military unit, paramilitary unit, police unit, self-defense unit, vigilante unit, citizen unit of the Nazi party or SS, government agency or office, extermination camp, concentration camp, prisoner of war camp, prison, labor camp, detention camp or transit camp, under the control or affiliated with:

    a. The Nazi Government of Germany? ☐ Yes ☐ No

    b. Any government in any area occupied by, allied with, or established with the assistance or cooperation of, the Nazi Government of Germany? ☐ Yes ☐ No

3. Have you at any time, anywhere, ever ordered, incited, assisted, or otherwise participated in the persecution of any person because of race, religion, national origin, or political opinion? ☐ Yes ☐ No

4. Have you ever left the United States to avoid being drafted into the U.S. Armed Forces? ☐ Yes ☐ No

5. Have you ever failed to comply with Selective Service laws? ☐ Yes ☐ No

    If you have registered under the Selective Service laws, complete the following information:

    Selective Service Number:_____ Date Registered:_____

    If you registered before 1978, also provide the following:

    Local Board Number:_____ Classification:_____

6. Did you ever apply for exemption from military service because of alienage, conscientious objections or other reasons? ☐ Yes ☐ No

7. Have you ever deserted from the military, air or naval forces of the United States? ☐ Yes ☐ No

8. Since becoming a permanent resident, have you ever failed to file a federal income tax return? ☐ Yes ☐ No

9. Since becoming a permanent resident, have you filed a federal income tax return as a nonresident or failed to file a federal return because you considered yourself to be a nonresident? ☐ Yes ☐ No

10 Are deportation proceedings pending against you, or have you ever been deported, or ordered deported, or have you ever applied for suspension of deportation? ☐ Yes ☐ No

11. Have you ever claimed in writing, or in any way, to be a United States citizen? ☐ Yes ☐ No

12. Have you ever:

    a. been a habitual drunkard? ☐ Yes ☐ No

    b. advocated or practiced polygamy? ☐ Yes ☐ No

    c. been a prostitute or procured anyone for prostitution? ☐ Yes ☐ No

    d. knowingly and for gain helped any alien to enter the U.S. illegally? ☐ Yes ☐ No

    e. been an illicit trafficker in narcotic drugs or marijuana? ☐ Yes ☐ No

    f. received income from illegal gambling? ☐ Yes ☐ No

    g. given false testimony for the purpose of obtaining any immigration benefit? ☐ Yes ☐ No

13. Have you ever been declared legally incompetent or have you ever been confined as a patient in a mental institution? ☐ Yes ☐ No

14. Were you born with, or have you acquired in same way, any title or order of nobility in any foreign State? ☐ Yes ☐ No

15. Have you ever:

    a. knowingly committed any crime for which you have not been arrested? ☐ Yes ☐ No

    b. been arrested, cited, charged, indicted, convicted, fined or imprisoned for breaking or violating any law or ordinance excluding traffic regulations? ☐ Yes ☐ No

(If you answer yes to 15 , in your explanation give the following information for each incident or occurrence the **city**, **state**, and **country**, where the offense took place, the **date** and **nature** of the offense, and the **outcome** or **disposition** of the case).

Part 8. Allegiance to the U.S.

If your answer to any of the following questions is **"NO"**, attach a full explanation:

    1. Do you believe in the Constitution and form of government of the U.S.? ☐ Yes ☐ No

    2. Are you willing to take the full Oath of Allegiance to the U.S.? (see instructions) ☐ Yes ☐ No

    3. If the law requires it, are you willing to bear arms on behalf of the U.S.? ☐ Yes ☐ No

    4. If the law requires it, are you willing to perform noncombatant services in the Armed Forces of the U.S.? ☐ Yes ☐ No

    5. If the law requires it, are you willing to perform work of national importance under civilian direction? ☐ Yes ☐ No

Form N-400 (Rev 07/17/91)N

Part 9. Memberships and organizations.

A. List your present and past membership in or affiliation with every organization, association, fund, foundation, party, club, society, or similar group in the United States or in any other place. Include any military service in this part. If none, write "none". Include the name of organization, location, dates of membership and the nature of the organization. If additional space is needed, use separate paper.

_____

_____

_____

_____

Part 10. Complete only if you checked block " C " in Part 2.

How many of your parents are U.S. citizens? ☐ One ☐ Both (Give the following about one U.S. citizen parent:)

Family Name	Given Name	Middle Name

Address

Basis for citizenship:
☐ Birth
☐ Naturalization Cert. No.

Relationship to you (check one): ☐ natural parent   ☐ adoptive parent
☐ parent of child legitimated after birth

If adopted or legitimated after birth, give date of adoption or, legitimation: *(month/day/year)* _____

Does this parent have legal custody of you? ☐ Yes ☐ No

(Attach a copy of relating evidence to establish that you are the child of this U.S. citizen and evidence of this parent's citizenship.)

Part 11. Signature. *(Read the information on penalties in the instructions before completing this section).*

I certify or, if outside the United States, I swear or affirm, under penalty of perjury under the laws of the United States of America that this application, and the evidence submitted with it, is all true and correct. I authorize the release of any information from my records which the Immigration and Naturalization Service needs to determine eligibility for the benefit I am seeking.

Signature   **Date**

_____

Please Note: If you do not completely fill out this form, or fail to submit required documents listed in the instructions, you may not be found eligible for naturalization and this application may be denied.

Part 12. Signature of person preparing form if other than above. *(Sign below)*

I declare that I prepared this application at the request of the above person and it is based on all information of which I have knowledge.

Signature	Print Your Name	Date

Firm Name
and Address

DO NOT COMPLETE THE FOLLOWING UNTIL INSTRUCTED TO DO SO AT THE INTERVIEW

I swear that I know the contents of this application, and supplemental pages 1 through_____, that the corrections, numbered 1 through_____, were made at my request, and that this amended application, is true to the best of my knowledge and belief.

Subscribed and sworn to before me by the applicant.

_____
(Examiner's Signature)   Date

_____
(Complete and true signature of applicant)

FEDERAL BUREAU OF INVESTIGATION
UNITED STATES DEPARTMENT OF JUSTICE
WASHINGTON, D.C. 20537
APPLICANT

1. LOOP

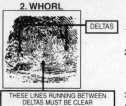

CENTER OF LOOP

DELTA

THE LINES BETWEEN CENTER OF LOOP AND DELTA MUST SHOW

2. WHORL

DELTAS

THESE LINES RUNNING BETWEEN DELTAS MUST BE CLEAR

3. ARCH

ARCHES HAVE NO DELTAS

TO OBTAIN CLASSIFIABLE FINGERPRINTS

1. USE BLACK PRINTER'S INK.
2. DISTRIBUTE INK EVENLY ON INKING SLAB.
3. WASH AND DRY FINGERS THOROUGHLY.
4. ROLL FINGERS FROM NAIL TO NAIL, AND AVOID ALLOWING FINGERS TO SLIP.
5. BE SURE IMPRESSIONS ARE RECORDED IN CORRECT ORDER.
6. IF AN AMPUTATION OR DEFORMITY MAKES IT IMPOSSIBLE TO PRINT A FINGER, MAKE A NOTATION TO THAT EFFECT IN TH THE INDIVIDUAL FINGER BLOCK.
7. IF SOME PHYSICAL CONDITION MAKE SIT IMPOSSIBLE TO OBTAIN PERFECT IMPRESSIONS, SUBMIT THE BEST THAT CAN BE OBTAINED WITH A MEMO STAPLED TO THE CARD EXPLAINING THE CIRCUMSTANCES.
8. EXAMINE THE COMPLETED PRINTS TO SEE IF THEY CAN BE CLASSIFIED, BEARING IN MIND THAT MOST FINGERPRINTS FALL IN T THE PATTERNS SHOWN ON THIS CARD)OTHER PATTERNS OCCUR INFREQUENTLY AND ARE NOT SHOWN HERE).

THIS CARD FOR USE BY: **LEAVE THIS SPACE BLANK**

1. LAW ENFORCEMENT AGENCIES IN FINGERPRINTING APPLICANTS FOR LAW ENFORCEMENT POSITIONS.*
2. OFFICIALS OF STATE AND LOCAL GOVERNMENTS FOR PURPOSES OF EMPLOYMENT, LICENSING, AND PERM,ITS, AS AUTHORIZED BY STATE STATUTES AND APPROVED BY TH ATTORNEY GENERAL OF THE UNTIED STATES. LOCAL AND COUNTY ORDINANCES. UNLESS SPECIFICALLY BASED ON APPLICABLE STATE STATUTES DO NOT SATISFY THIS REQUIREMENT.*
3. U.S. GOVERNMENT AGENCIES AND OTHER ENTITIES REQUIRED BY FEDERAL LAW.**
4. OFFICIALS OF FEDERALLY CHARTED OR INSURED BANKING INSTITUTIONS TO PROMOTE OR MAINTAIN THE SECURITY OF THOSE INSTITUTIONS.

INSTRUCTIONS:

*1. PRINTS MUST FIRST BE CHECKED THROUGH THE APPROPRIATE STATE IDENTIFICATION BUREAU, AND ONLY THOSE FINGERPRINTS FOR WHICH NO DISQUALIFYING RECORD HAS BEEN FOUND LOCALLY SHOULD BE SUBMITTED FOR FBI SEARCH.
2. PRIVACY ACT OF 1974 (P.L. 93-579) REQUIRES THAT FEDERAL, STATE, OR LOCAL AGENCIES INFORM INDIVIDUALS WHOSE SOCIAL SECURITY NUMBER IS REQUESTED WHETHER SUCH DISCLOSURE IS MANDATORY OR VOLUNTARY, BASIS OF AUTHORITY FOR SUCH SOLICITATION, AND USES WHICH WILL BE MADE OF IT.
**3. IDENTITY OF PRIVATE CONTRACTORS SHOULD BE SHOWN IN SPACE "EMPLOYER AND ADDRESS". THE CONTRIBUTOR IS THE NAME OF THE AGENCY SUBMITTING THE FINGERPRINT CARD TO THE FBI.
4. FBI NUMBER, IF KNOWN, SHOULD ALWAYS BE FURNISHED IN THE APPROPRIATE SPACE. MISCELLANEOUS NO. - RECORD: OTHER ARMED FORCES NO., PASSPORT NO. (PP), ALIEN REGISTRATION NO. (AR), PORT SECURITY CARD NO. (PS), SELECTIVE SERVICE NO. (22), VETERANS' ADMINISTRATION CLAIM NO. (VA).

FD-258 (REV. 12-29-82)   U.S. GPO:1994—301-155/80095

APPLICANT

LEAVE BLANK

SIGNATURE OF PERSON FINGERPRINTED

RESIDENCE OF PERSON FINGERPRINTED

| DATE | SIGNATURE OF OFFICIAN TAKING FINGERPRINTS] |

EMPLOYER AND ADDRESS

REASON FINGERPRINTED

TYPE OR PRINT ALL INFORMATION IN BLACK

| LAST NAME NAM | FIRST NAME   MIDDLE NAME |

FBI   LEAVE BLANK

ALIASES AKA   O R I

DATE OF BIRTH DOB
MONTH   DAY   YEAR

| CITIZENSHIP CTZ | SEX | RACE | HGT | WGT | EYES | HAIR | PLACE OF BIRTH POB |

YOUR NO OCA

FBI NO FBI

ARMED FORCES NO NMU

SOCIAL SECURITY NO. SOC

MISCELLANEOUS NO MNU

LEAVE BLANK

CLASS _____

REF. _____

| 1. R. THUMB | 2. R. INDEX | 3. R. MIDDLE | 4. R. RING | 5. R. LITTLE |

| 6. L. THUMB | 7. L. INDEX | 8. L. MIDDLE | 9. L. RING | 10. L. LITTLE |

| LEFT FOUR FINGERS TAKEN SIMUTANEOUSLY | L. THUMB | R. THUMB | RIGHT FOUR FINGERS TAKEN SIMUTANEOUSLY |

100 Citizenship Study Questions

1. What are the colors of our flag?

2. How many stars are there in our flag?

3. What color are the stars of our flag?

4. What do the stars on the flag mean?

5. How many stripes are there in the flag?

6. What color are the stripes?

7. What do the stripes on the flag mean?

8. How many states are there in the Union?

9. What is the 4th of July?

10. What is the date of Independence Day?

11. Independence from whom?

12. What country did we fight during the Revolutionary War?

13. Who was the first President of the United States?

14. Who is the President of the United States today?

15. Who is the Vice President?

16. Who elects the President of the United States?

17. Who becomes President of the United States if the President should die?

18. For how long do we elect the President?

19. What is the Constitution?

20. Can the Constitution be changed?

21. What do we call a change to the Constitution?

22. How many changes or amendments are there to the Constitution?

23. How many branches are there in our government?

24. What are the three branches of our government?

25. What is the legislative branch of our government?

26. Who make the laws in the United States?

27. What is Congress?

28. What are the duties of Congress?

29. Who elects Congress?

30. How many senators are there in Congress?

31. Can you name the two senators from your state?

32. For how long do we elect each senator?

33. How many representatives are there in Congress?

34. For how long do we elect the representatives?

35. What is the executive branch of our government?

36. What is the judicial branch of our government?

37. What are the duties of the Supreme Court?

38. What is the supreme law of the United States?

39. What is the Bill of Rights?

40. What is the capital of your state?

41. Who is the current governor of you state?

42. Who becomes President of the United States if the President and Vice President should die?

43. Who is the Chief Justice of the Supreme Court?

44. Can you name the thirteen original states?

45. Who said, "Give me liberty or give me death!"?

46. Which countries were our principal allies during World War II?

47. What are the 49th and 50th states of the Union?

48. How many terms can a president serve?

49. Who was Martin Luther King, Jr.?

50. Who is the head of your local government?

51. According to the Constitution, a person must meet certain requirements in order to be eligible to become President. Name one of these requirements.

52. Why are there 100 Senators in the Senate?

53. Who selects the Supreme Court Justices?

54. How many Supreme Court Justices are there?

55. Why did the Pilgrims come to America?

56. What is the head executive of a state government called?

57. What is the head executive of a city government called?

58. What holiday was celebrated for the first time by the American colonists?

59. Who was the main writer of the Declaration of Independence?

60. When was the Declaration of Independence adopted?

61. What is the basic belief of the Declaration of Independence?

62. What is the national anthem of the United States?

63. Who wrote the Star-Spangled Banner?

64. Where does freedom of speech come from?

65. What is the minimum voting age in the United Sates?

66. Who signs bills into law?

67. What is the highest court in the United States?

68. Who was President during the Civil War?

69. What did the Emancipation Proclamation do?

70. What special group advises the President?

71. Which President is called the "Father of our Country"?

72. What is the 50th state of the Union (U.S.)?

73. Who helped the Pilgrims in America?

74. What is the name of the ship that brought the Pilgrims to America?

75. What were the 13 original states of the U.S. called?

76. Name 3 rights or freedoms guaranteed by the Bill of Rights.

77. Who has the power to declare war?

78. Name one amendment which guarantees or addresses voting rights.

79. Which President freed the slaves?

80. In what year was the Constitution written?

81. What are the first 10 amendments to the Constitution called?

82. Name one purpose of the United Nations.

83. Where does the Congress meet?

84. Whose rights are guaranteed by the Constitution and the Bill of Rights?

85. What is the introduction to the Constitution called?

86. Name one benefit of being a citizen of the United States?

87. What is the most important right granted to U.S. citizens?

88. What is the United States Capitol?

89. What is the White House?

90. Where is the White House located?

91. What is the name of the President's official home?

92. Name one right guaranteed by the first amendment.

93. Who is the Commander in Chief of the U.S. Military?

94. Which President was the first Commander in Chief of the U.S. military?

95. In what month do we vote for the President?

96. In what month is the new President inaugurated?

97. How many times may a Senator be re-elected?

98. How many times may a Congressman be re-elected?

99. What are the 2 major political parties in the U.S. today?

100. How many states are there in the United States?

Student Objectives and Target Terms for each Lesson

LESSON 1
Students will be able to describe the U.S. flag using vocabulary that requires knowledge of numbers and colors. Students will be able to discuss and write about concepts relevant to the flag.
Target Words: Flag, Colony, State

LESSON 2
Learners will recognize the Pledge of Allegiance and be able to explain that it is a promise to be loyal to the United States.
Target Words: Pledge, Republic, Indivisible, Liberty, Justice, Allegiance, Symbol

LESSON 3
Students will be able to describe some events that led to the Revolutionary War, such as a desire for a free country and against unfair taxation. Students will be able to name Thomas Jefferson as the main author of the Declaration of Independence, George Washington as the leader of the American army and first president, and the Liberty Bell as a symbol of Independence.
Target Words: Revolutionary War, England, English, Tax(es), Colonist, Paul Revere, Establish, Terms, Serves, Advises, Cabinet, System, Thomas Jefferson, John Adams, Benjamin Franklin, Declaration of Independence, Principal Writer, Wrote, Create, Honors, Memorial, Continental Congress, Individuals, Document, Liberty Bell, Rang, Announce, Independence Hall

LESSON 4
Students will be able to explain that the Constitution, including the Bill of Rights, is the supreme law of the United States. Students will be able to name some of the provisions of each.
Target Words: Constitution, Supreme Law, Agree, Preamble, Bill of Rights, Power, Amendments, Rights, Trial, Jury, Lawyer, Testify, Court of Law, Protects, Cruel, Unusual Punishment, Citizen, Close, Members, Vote, Apply, Federal

LESSON 5
Students will be able to identify the Confederacy and Union as participants in the Civil War, slavery as one of the causes of the war, and Abraham Lincoln as the President and signer of the Emancipation Proclamation.
Target Words: Civil War, Southern, Northern, Divided, Half, United, Slavery, Free/Freedom, Confederacy, Union, Commanded, Abraham Lincoln, Sixteenth (16th), Emancipation, Proclamation

LESSON 6
Students will be able to identify U.S. allies during World Wars I and II, recognize Franklin D. Roosevelt as President during World War II and the Depression, and understand the Great Depression as a worldwide time of economic hardship.
Target Words: Europe, World War I, To Go To War, Allies, Great Depression, World War II, Dictators, United Nations, Economy, Failed, Franklin D. Roosevelt, Homeless

LESSON 7
Students will be able to state that the United States became involved in Vietnam to fight communism; recognize that John F. Kennedy was President in the early years of U.S. involvement; and that when Kennedy was assassinated, Vice President Lyndon Johnson became President.
Target Words: Vietnam, Communist, Communism, South Vietnam, North Vietnam, John F. Kennedy, Assassinated, Lyndon Johnson, Vietnam Memorial, Honors

LESSON 8
Students will be able to identify the Pilgrims and Native Americans and state the reason for the first Thanksgiving.
Target Words: Celebrate, Fourth, Thursday, Holiday, Thanksgiving, Pilgrims, Mayflower, Sailed/Sailing, Harvest, Suffered, Hunt

LESSON 9
Students will be able to relate Independence Day to the signing of the Declaration of Independence on July 4, 1776, and identify Francis Scott Key as the writer of our national anthem.
Target Words: Fourth of July, Celebrations, Fireworks, Picnics, Parade, Signing, July 4th, Banner, Anthem, Francis Scott Key

LESSON 10
Students will be able to describe the following American holidays: Presidents' Day, Martin Luther King, Jr., Day, Memorial Day, Veterans Day, Labor Day, and Columbus Day. Students will also be able to name the dates of the celebrations.
Target Words: Events, History, Holiday, February, January, Guaranteed, Civil Rights, Martin Luther King, Jr., Memorial Day, May, Individuals, Veteran(s), Armed Forces, Labor, September, Workers, Christopher Columbus, October, Arrived

LESSON 11
Students will be able to name the legislative branch as one of the 3 branches of the U.S. government and identify Congress as the legislative branch. Students will also be able to describe the function of Congress as making laws; identify some of the laws under the domain of Congress; state that the people elect members of Congress; and differentiate between the House and Senate in terms of total number of members and length of service.
Target Words: Branch(es), Legislature, Congress, Capitol, Lawmakers, Senate, House of Representatives, Naturalized Citizen, Representative(s), Senate/Senator(s), Trade, Approve, Chooses, Chosen, To Pass Laws, Elected

LESSON 12
Students will be able to name the executive branch as one of the 3 branches of the U.S. government; name some of the duties of the President, Vice president, and Cabinet; state the length of the President's term; explain the order of succession to the presidency.
Target Words: Executive Branch, Chief Executive, Enforces, White House, Bills, Main, Duty, Presides, Cabinet, To Sign a Bill into Law, Commander in Chief, Vice-President, Armed Services, Terms, Next, Presidential, Inaugurated, Requirements

LESSON 13
Students will be able to name the judicial branch as one of the 3 branches of the U.S. government; identify the Supreme Court as the judicial branch; state the function of the Supreme Court; describe the position of Chief Justice and give the number of associate judges.
Target Words: Judicial, Judges, Justice, Supreme Court, Interpret, City, States, Federal, Decision(s), Majority, Disagrees, Serve, Able, To Hear a Case (or Cases), To Fire, Chief Justice

LESSON 14
Students will be able to recognize that the U.S. government includes federal, state, and local levels; identify some specific domains of state law; recognize capital cities as seats of state government; identify capital cities of several key states.
Target Words: State, Own, Laws, Rules, Government, Education, Roads, Marriage, Legislators, Governor, To Pass a Law

LESSON 15
Students will be able to identify the two main political parties in the U.S. and identify their local and state government officials.
Target Words: Political, Parties, Compete, Republic, Republican, Democratic, Democrat, Democracy, Similar, Goals, Protect, Welfare, Achieving, Meetings, Conventions, Purpose, Policy/Policies

ANSWER KEY

LESSON 1
Page 3, Copy It Down - Have each student copy the sentences in this exercise.
Page 5, Figure It Out - 1. stars 2. white and blue 3. stripes
Dialogue - S1: States; S2: thirteen; S1: colonies; S2: flag; S1: fifty

LESSON 2
Page 8, Copy It Down - Have each student copy the sentences in this exercise.
Page 9, Figure It Out - Matching: 1. pledge/promise 2. allegiance/loyalty 3. Republic/form of government 4. liberty/freedom 5. justice/fairness 6. indivisible/cannot be divided
Fill in the Blanks - pledge; allegiance; Republic; indivisible; liberty; justice

LESSON 3
Page 17, Copy It Down - Have each student copy the sentences in this exercise.
Page 19, Figure It Out - Dialogue 1 - S1: Revolutionary; S1: Washington; S2: president; S1: Father; Dialogue 2 - S1: Independence; S2: England; S1: Declaration; S2: Jefferson; S1: equal

LESSON 4
Page 24, Figure It Out - Across:
1. Preamble 5. Constitution 6. Vote 7. Close; Down:
2. Amendment 3. Rights 4. Power

LESSON 5
Page 28, Figure It Out - Circle the correct answer: 1. no 2. yes 3. yes 4. yes 5. no
Complete the Puzzle: Across: 1. Emancipation 4. United; Down 2. Civil 3. Lee

LESSON 6
Page 32, Figure It Out - Circle the Correct Answer: 1. no 2. no 3. yes 4. no 5. yes 6. no 7. yes 8. yes

LESSON 7
Page 35, Figure It Out - Matching: 1. South Vietnam 2. North Vietnam 3. John F. Kennedy 4. 1960 5. 1963 6. Lyndon Johnson 7. 1973

LESSON 8
Page 40, Figure It Out - Complete the Puzzle: Across: 2. Native Americans 4. Pilgrims 5. Freedom; Down: 1. Dinner 2. November 3. Mayflower

LESSON 9
Page 44, Figure It Out - Complete the Puzzle: Across: 3. Declaration 5. Independence 6. July ; Down: 1. Holiday 2. Anthem 4. Banner

LESSON 10
Page 47, Copy It Down - Have each student copy the sentences in this exercise.
Page 49, Figure It Out - Circle the dates of the holidays: Labor Day/ September 4; Veterans Day/November 11; Presidents' Day/February 20; Martin Luther King, Jr., Day/January 16; Columbus Day/October 9; Memorial Day/ May 29

LESSON 11
Page 54, Copy It Down - Have each student copy the sentences in this exercise.
The Congress:
House of Representatives:
1; 435; 2; 25;
Senate: 2; 100; 6; 30
Page 56, Figure It Out - Short Answers: 1. Congress 2. House of Representatives, Senate 3. The people 4. 100 5. 435 6. 2 years
7. 6 years

LESSON 12
Page 60, Figure It Out - 1. B 2. A 3. A 4. B 5. A
Circle the Correct Words: 1. four 2. one time 3. 35 4. born 5. November 6. January
Lesson 13
Page 63, Copy It Down - Have each student copy the sentences in this exercise.
Page 64, Figure It Out -
A. Executive branch is the picture in the middle B. Legislative branch is the picture on the left
C. Judicial branch is the picture on the right

LESSON 14
Page 68, Copy It Down - Have each student copy the sentences in this exercise.
Page 69, Figure It Out -
1. Massachusetts/Boston
2. New York/Albany
3. Ohio/Columbus
4. Georgia/Atlanta
5. Florida/Tallahassee
6. Louisiana/Baton Rouge
7. Texas/Austin
8. New Mexico/Santa Fe
9. Arizona/Phoenix
10. California/Sacramento
LESSON 15
Page 72, Copy It Down - answers will vary
Page 73, Figure It Out - 1. republic 2. Democrats 3. mayor 4. elephant 5. donkey 6. protect

100 CITIZENSHIP QUESTIONS
1. Red, white and blue; 2. 50; 3. White; 4. One for each state in the union; 5. 13; 6. Red and white; 7. They represent the original thirteen states; 8. 50; 9. Independence Day; 10. July 4th; 11. England; 12. England; 13. George Washington; 14. Bill Clinton; 15. Al Gore; 16. The electoral college; 17. Vice President; 18. Four years; 19. The supreme law of the land; 20. Yes; 21. Amendment; 22. 26; 23. 3; 24. Legislative, executive, and judicial; 25. Congress; 26. Congress; 27. The Senate and The House of Representatives; 28. To make laws; 29. The people; 30. 100; 31. Answers will vary; 32. 6 years; 33. 435; 34. 2 years; 35. The President, Cabinet, and departments under the cabinet members; 36. The Supreme Court; 37. To interpret laws; 38. The Constitution; 39. The first 10 amendments of the Constitution; 40. Answers will vary; 41. Answers will vary; 42. Speaker of the House of Representatives; 43. William Rehnquist;

44. Connecticut, New Hampshire, New York, New Jersey, Massachusetts, Pennsylvania, Delaware, Virginia, North Carolina, South Carolina, Georgia, Rhode Island, and Maryland; 45. Patrick Henry; 46. United Kingdom, Canada, Australia, New Zealand, France, Russia, China; 47. Hawaii and Alaska; 48. 2; 49. A civil rights leader; 50. Answers will vary; 51. Must be a natural born citizen of the United States; must be at least 35 years old by the time he/she will serve; must have lived in the United States for at least 14 years; 52. 2 from each state; 53. Appointed by President; 54. 9; 55. For religious freedom; 56. Governor; 57. Mayor; 58. Thanksgiving; 59. Thomas Jefferson; 60. July 4, 1776; 61. That all men are created equal; 62. The Star-Spangled Banner; 63. Francis Scott Key; 64. The Bill of Rights; 65. 18; 66. The President; 67. The Supreme Court; 68. Abraham Lincoln; 69. Freed many slaves; 70. The Cabinet; 71. George Washington; 72. Hawaii; 73. The American Indians (Native Americans); 74. The *Mayflower*; 75. The Colonies; 76. [1. The right of freedom of speech, press, religion, peaceable assembly and requesting change of government. [2. The right to bear arms (the right to have weapons or own a gun, though subject to certain regulations). [3. The government may not quarter, or house, soldiers in the people's homes during peacetime without the people's consent. [4. The government may not search or take a person's property without a warrant. [5. A person may not be tried twice for the same crime and does not have to testify against him/herself. [6. A person charged with a crime still has some rights, such as the right to a trial and to have a lawyer. [7. The right to trial by jury in most cases. [8. Protects people against excessive or unreasonable fines or cruel and unusual punishment. [9. the people have rights other than those mentioned in the Constitution. [10. Any power not given to the federal government by the Constitution is a power of either the state or the people.]; 77. The Congress; 78. 15th, 19th, 24th, and 26th; 79. Abraham Lincoln; 80. 1787; 81. The Bill of Rights; 82. For countries to discuss and try to resolve world problems; to provide economic aid to many countries; 83. In the Capitol in Washington, D.C.; 84. All citizens and noncitizens living in the U.S.; 85. The Preamble; 86. Obtain federal government jobs; travel with a U.S. Passport; petition for close relative to come to the U.S. to live; 87. The right to vote; 88. The place where Congress meets; 89. The President's official home; 90. Washington, D.C. (1600 Pennsylvania Avenue, N.W.); 91. The White House; 92. Freedom of: speech, press, religion, peaceable assembly, and requesting change of the government; 93. The President; 94. George Washington; 95. November; 96. January; 97. There is no limit. 98. There is no limit; 99. Democratic and Republican; 100. 50.